Captain Timmy
&
the Bobbing Barrel

by
Robert Campbell

www.robertcampbell.me

Books for Wains, Kids & Children by Robert Campbell

www.wkc.news.blog

Other Books

"Sled Down"

"George and the Elephant"

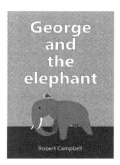

With Profound thanks and gratitude to:
Dr Bernadette Power (Consultant Paediatrician -
Letterkenny University Hospital)

Dr Michael Roynane (Consultant Anaesthetist- ICU
Letterkenny University Hospital)

The Nurses and staff of the Children's Ward,
Letterkenny University Hospital

Ambulance & Paramedic Team Letterkenny
University Hospital

Dr Ronan Leahy (Consultant Paediatric
Immunologist, Crumlin Childrens' Hospital, Dublin)

Dr Adam James (Consultant Cardiologist, Crumlin
Childrens' Hospital, Dublin

The Consultants, doctors, ICU nurses and staff of
PICU1
(Paediatric Intensive Care Unit One, Crumlin
Childrens' Hospital, Dublin)

also

Mark Patterson, BBC Radio Foyle
On helping to raise awareness of Paediatric
Inflammatory Multisystem Syndrome (PIMS)

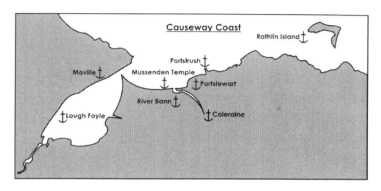

Causeway Coast

Rathlin Island
Portrush
Mussenden Temple
Portstewart
Moville
River Bann
Coleraine
Lough Foyle

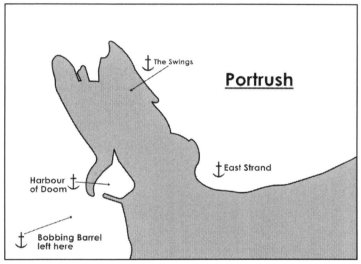

The Swings

Portrush

East Strand

Harbour
of Doom

Bobbing Barrel
left here

The First Bit

Captain Timmy, what a guy! He was brave, furious, adventurous, foolhardy, slightly clumsy, and he didn't always have the greatest of ideas. But he, along with his ragtag crew were undoubtedly some of the good guys in the pirate world.

These kinds of ripping yarns are meant to begin with heroic battles on the high seas. The kind of thing where there's roaring waves, boisterous waters, stellar victories, desert islands, treasure maps, and treasure chests jam-packed full of shiny gold and sparkly gems.

But please don't get your hopes up, and definitely do not conjure up in the recesses of your mind, life and death struggles in the middle of the freezing cold Atlantic Ocean!

The only freezing cold Atlantic around here is off the east Strand! The absence of Bermuda shorts lets you know the water is cold. And if you look carefully, you will notice that all the surfers are wrapped up like Arctic seals in their winter wet suits. This is not Hawaii nor is it the Gold Coast. This is the north coast, just as beautiful, but not as warm!

Anyhow, our crew, Captain Timmy's crew, have managed to do something very silly! Something they don't even know about yet - they've lost their boat! Yip, that's right they have managed to lose a honking great big Pirate ship.

Pirate Terrance, aka Red Beard, that notorioussssssssssssssssssssly unreliable trainee pirate hadn't bothered to check his knots, and the Bobbing Barrel had bobbed away!

They had managed to safely cross the Atlantic Ocean, and arrived safely at Portrush. You see they'd come to the Port seeking provisions and pleasure, otherwise known as fish & chips and then a run round Barrys!

Captain Timmy, (who considered himself to be a rather cultured type of guy) wanted a game of golf on The Links but Grey Beard, Captain Timmy's right-hand-pirate wasn't so sure this was a good idea. He was painfully aware of their last, and might I add, disastrous incursion onto the hallowed turf of the Royal Course.

Paying green fees never entered the pirates' minds. Instead they considered it their bounden duty to sneak onto the course from the sand dunes. However this plan was an utter failure as they got caught straightaway. Having been caught, they were politely asked to leave. With profuse apologies and many farfetched excuses, they made their way back onto the sand dunes. But the green keeper who was a very good judge of character, and didn't trust them one little bit, hid in the bushes. So as soon as they reappeared over the fence, they were promptly thrown out again. He was less polite this time, and they were thrown out again...and again... and again, until the police were called and they had to run for it!

They didn't want a trip to the beautiful red bricked building at Metropol Corner (if you didn't get *"your teenage kicks"* cruising the Port, and with every lap realising more and more that *"a good heart was hard to find"*), that's the police station!

Anyhow, on this visit, once they had come out of Barrys, with heads spinning and stomachs just a little bit queasy, and with sufficient victual taken, they all agreed that it was time to head back to the Bobbing Barrel. Miraculously they took the top road (remember young pirates it's always much easier to defend high ground).

But let's be honest, they went that way because all the cool surfing shops are up there! Captain

Timmy had once managed to get something really hip and better still really cheap from one of the cool shops! But this time they were out of luck, even after some very humiliating haggling by Captain Timmy!

Empty handed they headed to the harbour. When they rounded the corner, and looked down on it, it was a scene of utter pandemonium.

The Second Bit

Grey Beard was the only one amongst them with any form of situational awareness. It's something that's ultra important to piratey sort of people, well something that should be ultra important to piratey sort of people!

He was the only one to notice it...and what he noticed is the substance of this story.

He noticed it was gone! The ship was gone! Their pirate ship was gone! It was no longer there! It was no longer where it should have been! It was no longer where they had left it!

Once this rather important, and rather obvious fact had been relayed to the other pirates (pirates who were all standing right beside Grey Beard and all looking in the same direction...once they saw, well actually, once they *didn't* see it, because it wasn't there), they were enraged.

They were so vexed in fact that they drew their weapons. Out came the swords, the cudgels, the sticks, the flintlock pistols, a comb and a piece of chalk.

We need to explain the piece of chalk. Once, in the Port of Larne, Pirate Tam had been told to practice drawing his weapon. So taking the instruction very seriously, though not understanding what it actually meant, he'd gone up and down the Main Street drawing weapons using various pieces of coloured chalk. This only came to an end after a Middle Eastern battle, that is, this only came to an end after an argument with a very official looking person from Mid and East Antrim Council. But Pirate Tam had not learned his lesson and from that moment on he always remembered to bring his chalk with him...just in case he ever got another chance to draw his weapon!

Pirate Terence, aka Red Beard (who should not be confused with Pirate Terry, because they are different people) waved his comb above his head in the most furious possible manner. It wasn't a deadly weapon, but it was a very annoying weapon, one that when operated properly could flick you very hard on the backside with a great whack.

But before any of the weapons could be used, Grey Beard, overruling Captain Timmy, roared, "*Men, put your weapons away!*"

Mightily relieved Captain Timmy asked, "*Have you spotted the ship?*"

"*No*", replied Grey Beard, "*but I have spotted three police wagons stuck in the traffic down by the life boat station, and they've got their blue flashing lights on, and I would bet they're heading for the harbour!*"

With weapons re-sheathed, hidden, and put away they stood looking down into the harbour. Pirate Terry, who is not to be confused with Pirate Terence, was the first to speak. *"Pirates"* he said in a most serious tone. They all listened intently. *"Pirates, has anyone got a plaster?"*

Whilst re-sheathing his sword Pirate Terry hadn't paid enough attention and had cut his finger! Once first aid had been rendered their full attention returned to gazing down into the harbour mouth.

They could see that it really was gone and was nowhere to be seen. It had vanished into thin air, and the mooring was empty!

They all presumed the same presumption - that the Bobbing Barrel had, without the least shadow of doubt, been the victim of pirates' shenanigans.

As they looked they started to notice something else. The harbour was full of exceptionally angry boat owners. These furious folk stood around the harbour wall, gathered in deadly huddles. Some were very close to the edge, so angry they didn't notice just how close they were to the edge. Clearly someone, or something had poked the apple of their eye, and they were very unhappy.

The pirates then made another observation. The normally neat rows of boats were no longer neat rows. They appeared to have been bashed, banged and knocked all over the place, by something that could bash, bang and knock them all over the place!

At this point their training kicked in, along with their nosiness. They needed, and indeed wanted to know what exactly had happened. The only way to do this was to go to the harbour and find out for themselves.

The Third Bit

The traffic was terrible, all the rubber-neckers
had managed to block the town. As these nosy
drivers arrived at the harbour they slowed right
down and had a good auld gawk before they
drove up the hill (though they couldn't see
much)! This meant that the police and pirates
arrived at the harbour at the same moment!

Two of the police wagons turned into the harbour
(that is, into the harbour car park...the water
contained enough wreckage already!). At the
gates, just as the third police wagon was about to
do the same, a bangin' tune from the '90s came
on the wireless. It was a song they hadn't heard

for ages. So they 'missed' the entrance and took another lap of the town.

One of the two shiny new police wagons that had made it into the harbour car park had not completely stopped moving when the sergeant decided it was a good idea to jump out. This is dangerous as he was about to find out! The sergeant caught his foot on the seatbelt. He stumbled, then stumbled forward, desperately trying not to fall, all the time pretending that he wanted to run forward unsteadily! Somehow he managed not to collapse. Then, with balance finally restored, he walked forward pretending it had never happened.

As the sergeant went over to a group of furious looking boat owners to start his investigations, their conversation fell silent. They'd seen him nearly fall. Normally they would have ribbed him about his acrobatic exit from the shiny new police wagon, but they were so cross because of their damaged boats they said nothing! The sergeant thought no one had seen his little trip -

that is his staggering and lurching about the place - so he felt pretty proud of himself!

He asked, *"So what's been happening here then?"* The least furious of the boat owners replied, *"Two boats have been sunnnn..."* A horrible gurgling sound interrupted him. This awful noise was the result of a perpendicular boat disappearing below the water! The boat owner continued reasonably calmly given the situation, *"Three boats have been sunk, and three others badly damaged by some large, ugly runaway thing that crashed into them and then drifted off!"*

Captain Timmy and Grey Beard had sneaked into the edge of the group. Realisation was starting to dawn that the Bobbing Barrel was the cause of the damage to these wee small teeny boats. Once the sergeant had finished speaking to the angry boat owner, Captain Timmy made his way over. In a totally inappropriate, haughty voice he asked, *"Sir, was your small, and well, rather insignificantly proportioned pleasure craft struck by a*

magnificent vessel, one that was both swift and
deadly?"

With remarkable speed the boat owner regained
his anger, and he became much angrier than he
had been in the first place! He snapped at
Captain Timmy (and here we are only able to
give the sense of his words), that his brand new
£100k cruiser had nearly been destroyed, *"by a*
decrepit old wooden boat that didn't look fit for the
water!" Returning to the sense of his words, one
that its incompetent captain hadn't tied up
properly!

They also discovered, in the midst of his rant (a
rant they believed to be totally unnecessary,
given that his ship had only been hit and not
sunk), that the unfortunate incident had occurred
just as these pleasure boat sailors were about to
leave for a boat show in Bangor where they fully
expected to win section 1C. As Captain Timmy
opened his mouth to indignantly reply, Grey
Beard, rightly worried by what he might say,
pulled him away. Which was just as well, as he

was about to tell the boat owner that winning prizes isn't everything!

The reports were not good! The Bobbing Barrel had definitely caused the damage. Apparently it had drifted into the harbour, and then bashed, banged and knocked many unfortunate vessels all over the place. After this it had somehow drifted back out to sea. The ship was actually visible in the distance as it continued drifting away. Even the dangling rope was visible through a good set of binoculars. The very rope that should have stopped it from drifting into the harbour, hitting a pile of boats, sinking a few, and then drifting back out into the open sea.

Pirate Tam said, and probably not at the best time, *"At least the Bobbing Barrel is wooden!"* Wistfully Captain Timmy replied, *"Yes, a fine old wooden vessel."* Pirate Tam continued, when he really should have stopped, *"That's not what I meant. I meant it's wooden so it's biodegradable. At least when it sinks, it won't fill the seabirds or the little fishes stomachs with plastic and oil and all that dangerous sort of stuff."*

Obviously this was a good thing. Would you want your stomach filled with plastic, oil, and all that dangerous sort of stuff? However, this was not the best time to say it! Not noticing the Captain's reddening face, Pirate Tam continued, *"And if it doesn't break up when it hits the Skerries, it will give sea life a wonderful new home."* Then lapsing into the whispered voice of a natural history TV presenter, *"A wonderful eco-system for marine creatures to live in..."*

But before he could go on, Pirate Ted chimed in, inadvertently bringing them back to the real problem, *"And something new for the divers to gawk at, or salvage treasure from!"*

"Pirates," Grey Beard snapped abruptly. Then pointing out to sea he said, *"The boat hasn't sank!"* Obviously the boat hadn't sank, they could see it, they could see it bobbing and drifting about all by itself. He went on, *"In all likelihood it won't*

23

sink. The real danger is that it will run aground, or be captured by other pirates, or more likely impounded by the coast guard." Then, looking very grim, Grey Beard said, *"But we do need to do something, and do that something pretty quickly!"*

The Fourth Bit

While he was still gazing out to sea, someone appeared beside Captain Timmy. No one saw where he came from, not even Grey Beard. This small, well dressed person with a meticulous moustache just appeared. He wore a policeman's uniform. But his face was obscured below the peak of his hat, a hat that was pulled right down over his face.

It was only when he spoke that Captain Timmy realised someone was beside him. *"Well now, this is a right mess, isn't it, Sir?"* he said in the most ominous of tones. Captain Timmy didn't like it one little bit that someone had snuck up beside him, and he liked even less the tone in which he spoke. The little man continued, *"But don't you worry, we'll deal with the people who did this."*

Then, in what Captain Timmy took to be an accusation rather than a question, the little man asked, *"Was your boat damaged, Sir? Was it involved in the collision, Sir? What do you think happened here, Sir?"*

As the little man with the meticulous moustache spoke, Captain Timmy felt very hot, and strangely, his collar seemed to become very tight. But before Captain Timmy could reply, the little man continued, *"Do you know where we'll **not** catch them?"* This time he paused, and looked straight a Captain Timmy with a stare that seemed to look right through the nervous captain.

Having taken a deep breath, Captain Timmy timidly replied, *"Where's that?"* *"Coleraine,"* the little man with the meticulous moustache replied straightaway. *"We'll not get them in Coleraine. They definitely aren't in Coleraine, we know that for sure. In fact Sir, if they were at all wise, that's exactly where they would go to! But people like this never have the sense to go to Coleraine!"*

Bravely and with a terrible desperation that his voice would not become a nervous high pitched squeal, Captain Timmy asked, *"Why's that?"* The little man with the meticulous moustache, looking straight into Captain Timmy's eyes said, *"Because the kind of people who cause this kind of damage never think to go there."* And with that he was gone, though none of them saw him go.

Pirate Terrance, aka Red Beard, was standing with his head down. The seriousness of what he had done, okay not done, was starting to sink in, along with the realisation that the ship might sink. Grey Beard, the one who sees things, saw this and went over and stood beside him. After a moment or two he said, *"Red Beard, sometimes in life you just need to learn lessons."* Gloomily Pirate Terrance, aka Red Beard, looked up. Grey Beard went on, *"You just need to check over your work. It can be a nuisance, but look at the trouble it would have saved!"*

Grey Beard stopped speaking as, to use the vocabulary of the surfers, the Bobbing Barrel caught a wave and headed quickly towards the Skerries. Opened mouthed, which was not a pleasant sight, the pirates watched their ship hurtle towards the little islands.

With jerky hand and knee movements, they tried, as if they were watching a football match, to direct the ship away from the Skerries. It was close, very close, but phew, the Bobbing Barrel just missed the little islands! Smugly and with lots of unwarranted pride, the pirates wondered if it had been their jerky hand and knee movements that had made the ship miss.

Their joy, which was great, was short lived. Yes, the ship hadn't sunk or run aground, both of which are really important. But the Bobbing Barrel was free and once again at the mercy of the sea! They watched as it headed in the general direction of Portstewart. This was sort of okay, however, it would only take a change of the tide or a change of the wind and it would be away off across the Narrow Sea to Scotland. Or worse still, if it caught the right wave it could be in the middle of the Atlantic Ocean in no time at all! Captain Timmy and his crew slipped away to regroup, and to wonder what on earth to do next.

The Fifth Bit

Slippery! Now that is a great word to describe these pirates. I don't mean slippery like wet and soapy, like bath time slippery. No, I don't mean that kind of slippery. I mean these guys were slippery slippery. Except for the annual bath, that's when they were the other kind of slippery and not this kind of slippery.

No, these guys were clever and cunning, conniving and crafty, clumsy and calamitous. But they were most often the last two.

As they legged it, or as they preferred to put it, as they slipped away, the harbour was still in a state of pandemonium, a scene of mayhem, a place where bedlam abounded. Every good pirate knew this created two things: danger and opportunity. But on this occasion, it spelt out loudly and clearly only one thing: "D-A-N-G-E-R".

I want to let you into a secret. Mariners who have suddenly become submariners because some idiot let their ship drift away and sank their tied up boats, start to pay much more attention.

They start to ask awkward questions like:
"Who owned the junk heap of a ship that hit my boat?"
Or *"Who was sailing it?"*
Or *"Is it registered?"*
Or *"Has anyone seen it before?"*
Or *"Will they be looking for it?"*
Or *"Can we get their insurance details?"*
Or *"Was it on its way to a wrecker's yard?"*
Or *"Why was such a low class vessel moored anywhere near my boat in the first place?"*

No one noticed them go. That is no one noticed them go except a small well dressed man with a meticulous moustache who was still keeping a very close eye on them. But none of the pirates noticed him watching, even though they were watching to see if anyone was watching them! So that was a bit of a fail for their pirating skills!

Captain Timmy's crew considered themselves good slipper awayers! You see, over the years these guys had lots of practice. They'd slipped away having buried treasure. They'd slipped away having dug it back up. They'd slipped away very quickly having dug up someone else's treasure. They'd slipped away from naval frigates. They'd slipped away from other pirate ships. Now they could add to this illustrious list that they had slipped away from irate boat owners!

So as you can see these guys were good. Or at least they were slightly better than the average. But since there were so few pirates about nowadays, the average had become pretty low.

They mustered; they regrouped; that is they gathered at the swings up by the tennis courts. They needed to meticulously plan what they were going to do next. So, looking for a bright spot in the darkness, they heartily congratulated themselves on their heroic escape from *the Harbour of Chaos*, as they had started to call it!

At the swings and at a good distance from *the Harbour of Chaos*, in mid boast, Grey Beard brought them back down to earth with a bump. In a very gruff voice he snapped at them, "*Space X could have launched a rocket and fired it from Rathlin Island, and attracted less attention than we have!*" They thought he'd finished, well they hoped he'd finished, but he hadn't. He was only getting into his stride. "*And if they had, they wouldn't have lost the rocket, or crashed it into half a dozen satellites on the way up!*"

As they listened, they found themselves staring into the heavens. They really wanted to catch a glimpse of this lunar collision. Especially since they now believed the space race had moved from Cape Canaveral to Rathlin Island! Grey Beard shook his head, sighed deeply and stopped speaking. Even after all these years he was stunned by their utter stupidity!

As the crew hung around the swings, Captain Timmy and Grey Beard went for a walk. They clasped their hands behind their backs. They looked very serious, their faces grim. They didn't go very far, they couldn't go very far, they couldn't leave the crew alone. Dear knows what they would have gotten up to if left to their own devices!

The two lead pirates were realising just how bad it was to lose your ship! They were in a real tight spot. The only way out was to come up with a good plan, a real plan, a plan that might actually work. This weighed heavily on their minds. Deep in thought, their heads drooped.

Retrieving the Bobbing Barrel wouldn't be easy. Everything they needed to rescue the ship was on

the ship! Worst of all, the ship was bobbing
about at sea, and they had no idea where it was,
or where exactly it was bobbing to!

The Sixth Bit

The rest of the pirates weren't worried by the precarious nature of their future, not one little bit. That's because they didn't realise just how precarious it was! So, being merrily oblivious to their peril (something they should have been pretty interested in) and being as easily distracted as ever, they started a "who can swing the highest" competition.

Pirate Terrance, aka Red Beard couldn't work a swing and because of this he kept coming last. He didn't know to throw your feet forward on the way up, to throw them back on the way down, to move with the swing, and to hold on tight. On several occasions he'd toppled off and plopped onto the ground, much to the amusement of the other pirates. He'd leaned too far this way, or too far that way, and then before he could do anything to save himself he'd toppled off.

He didn't like toppling off, nor did he like the brays of laughter from the other pirates when he did fall. So when it was his turn again, he just sat there and wouldn't let anyone push him. Occasionally he made a strange erratic, wriggly sort of movement but it definitely wasn't the kind of movement you were meant to make! Firstly, this made him sad, then, and very quickly, it made him angry for he was a bad tempered sort.

Everyone else could use a swing. Everyone else could whoosh up and down. That is everyone except Pirate Terrance, aka Red Beard. He expected to be good, to be better than everyone else, and to achieve this without any practice! But he couldn't argue with a swing. He couldn't demand that it succumbed to his bad tempered will. If he didn't make it work, it wouldn't, and as he couldn't make it work, it didn't!

Sitting there, occasionally making his strange erratic wiggly sort of movement, he didn't want to be as good as the other pirates, the ones who could whoosh up and down, he wanted to be better than them. Wanting to be better than other people and wanting to be your best are not the same thing, and he hadn't learned that lesson yet.

***

The pirates were in a monumental mess. They had flunked something very simple: tying up your boat. It is doubtful if they had attacked the harbour in a full frontal assault, they could have caused as much damage and mayhem as they had! It was a fiasco, a deeply embarrassing fiasco; it was a muddle; it was a debacle; but above all it was a lost ship. Somewhere out there, bobbing about on the high sea was their pirate ship. They had managed to slip away from the harbour to the swings, but there was only so far a pirate could slip without a pirate ship!

The Bobbing Barrel, their lost ship, contained all their worldly goods. All their money and all their gold, for all there was of it! But along with these, there were all their treasure maps - treasure maps that had taken many years to gather up and were actually very important documents. There were also the special and secret shipping charts - the charts that you need to sail dangerous waters, evade capture and remain inconspicuous. Obviously they could have done with them now. There were also the top secret code books - ciphers and so on that you need for deciphering pirate communications; communications that you may well receive in perilous or dangerous times - times like now for instance. These were books that must never fall into the wrong hands, and if they ever did fall into the wrong hands whoever lost them would be in big, big trouble. Then there were all the highly detailed log books that in the wrong hands could get them into really deep water, if you pardon the pun. Not to mention all the special tools needed to keep the ship safe and seaworthy, like ropes for safely securing it! And last but not least, all the clandestine weapons that even James Bond would be jealous of!

Having thought of all that, amazingly the ship was actually the least important thing that they had lost! It could easily be replaced with another ship, a better ship, a newer ship. Well it could be easily replaced if they had their treasure maps, but as they hadn't, the finding and digging up of some treasure to pay for this new boat was going to prove a bit of a problem!

There was another thing. Captain Timmy belonged to the Pirates Guild. The pirates didn't know about this (except for Grey Beard who also belonged to the Pirate Guild) but that was where the problems really started. You see the rules of the Pirate Guild clearly stated that, "*the careless loss of treasure maps, shipping charts or code books will result in the immediate dishonourable expulsion of captain and crew.*" This meant that all of them, not just Captain Timmy, could be expelled from ever being a member of the Pirate Guild. They would no longer be pirates, and worse still, they would not be allowed to sail on pirate ships as members of a pirate crew!

The Seventh Bit

Pirate Terence, aka Red Beard, who as we have already mentioned couldn't work the swings, had gone for a little walk. Though unable to work a swing, he was able to accidently on purpose, if you know what I mean, overhear conversations he shouldn't be hearing. From this eavesdropping he caught something Captain Timmy said about them not being pirates anymore. At first he was a bit perplexed and confused by what he heard, but quickly, in fact nearly instantly, he let his thoughts run wild as he imagined not being a pirate. He imagined himself as a movie star. Next he was an obnoxious, highly paid, and averagely talented footballer. Then he was a TV presenter. Quickly he became a successful entrepreneur. Then best of all, the captain of his own ship. But with unusual insight he snapped out of it as he pondered the question, *"Would life really be good if everything changed that much?"*

Captain Timmy and Grey Beard had finally come up with a plan. It certainly wasn't their greatest plan ever. It definitely wasn't a plan that was guaranteed to work. In fact it was a pretty risky plan, a gamble, a shot in the dark. But it was all they had. There was no choice, so they had to run with it!

Captain Timmy walked back to the swings to inform the crew. The pirates paid no attention to him. Pirate Tam had already won the swinging up and down competition. With the rest of the crew standing watching, he zoomed up and down at an amazing speed. He was now just showing off, with some of the less gracious pirates hoping he would fall off! *"Hee hem"* Captain Timmy sounded. Again, no one paid any attention. *"Hee hem!"* he said with a deeper, louder guttural sound. Still no one paid any attention. *"Men!"* roared Grey Beard. They stopped, looked, listened, and became quiet. Well, all except Pirate Tam who continued to whizz up and down. It wasn't easy to stop suddenly when you were going at that kind of speed.

Now, having their attention, Captain Timmy announced to the Bobbing Barrel's crew in a commanding voice: *"Pirates, you must search your pockets and give me whatever money you have."*

On their last visit to Portrush - the occasion when they hadn't lost their ship - no restrictions had been imposed upon them. The captain had allowed them to go ashore, taking as much money as they liked with them. Actually Captain Timmy had never thought that they'd take, and then lose all their money in one day! He was shocked that evening when they came back home to the Bobbing Barrel with empty pockets and absolutely nothing to show for it! This time, much to the pirates' annoyance, Captain Timmy had put his foot down and severely limited the amount of cash they were allowed to take. Though, in all honesty it was still far too much!

So, with most of their money safely on the Bobbing Barrel (usually that would have been a good thing), there they stood with nearly empty pockets (which in these trying circumstances was a bad thing)! Eventually, all the meagre contents of their pockets were plopped down onto the picnic table. A few coins slipped through a crack and onto the ground, but once carefully retrieved, the money was counted. It came to the grand total of £21 and 54p, €3 and 22c, $4 and 95c, 1 Yen, 3 buttons, 12 washers, 4 screws and a bag of sweets. The bag of sweets was a horrible mess. In the heat and the sweat of the pocket, the sweets and the paper bag had fused together into a huge sticky blob.

The screws and washers were needed for the ship, so they weren't needed now, but they would be if they ever got it back. The Yen, the Euros and the US Dollars all needed to be changed into Sterling, so at this moment of time, they too were of no use. That left them with the grand total of £21 and 54 pence. And of course the sweets...if they ever could be pried off the paper; paper to which they were well and truly stuck!

Pirate Tattie asked Captain Timmy if he could have the sweets. Captain Timmy, whose thoughts were fully focused on retrieving the Bobbing Barrel, just handed them to him, which really wasn't a good idea! Straightaway Pirate Tattie started trying to pick the paper off, but it wasn't working for the whole thing was far too sticky. Then he had a brainwave. He would suck the paper off. If you've ever tried to do this, then you know where this story is headed!

After quite a bit of effort he managed to break off a lump! This slightly smaller gloppy lump he then popped into his mouth. He started to suck and rub it with his tongue. Very quickly the gloppy mess became a huge gooey, sticky, sugary, gloppy mess, all of which was contained within the confines of Pirate Tattie's mouth! It would be uncharitable to say that Pirate Tattie had a big mouth, but equally it would be untrue to say that it was small. But whatever size his mouth was, the gloppy mess had more than filled it! This was very unsafe! Eventually with Grey Beard's help, and just before he choked himself, the gooey, sticky, sugary, gloppy mess was spat into a tissue and dumped into the bin, along with the rest of the sweets.

When the commotion of the gloppy sweets was finally sorted, Captain Timmy informed the crew that they had not enough money. The only thing they could do was search through their pockets again, and really hope that they'd missed something the first time. So, they searched their jacket pockets. They searched their trouser pockets. They searched their front pockets. They searched their back pockets. They searched the funny wee pocket at the front of your jeans, the one that's only any use for a folded up fiver, tenner, or twenty pound note. They even searched their secret pockets. But for all this

searching the only thing they found was one
token for the amusements!

Well everyone searched their pockets except
Pirate Terrance, aka Red Beard, aka the loser of
the boat. He didn't need to. But before anyone
noticed he wasn't searching his pockets, Pirate
Tattie had a brain wave and shouted: *"Pirates, to
the swings!"* Captain Timmy glared at him.
*"That's not what you're meant to be doing, you're
meant to be searching your pockets!"* the captain
crossly reminded him. With the wind well and
truly taken out of his sails, and now sounding
more than a little dejected, he said, *"But Captain,
people always drop money at the swings."* *"Yes!"*
Captain Timmy yelled, much louder than he had
meant to. Then making the idea sound like his
own, he shouted the order, *"To the swings,
pirates!"*

Once there, the pirates assumed the 'swing as
high as you can' competition would resume.
They were a little disappointed when they
realised it hadn't and that they were there to

search for money. Anyhow, under the swings, they found a £1 coin, two 50 pence pieces, three 20 pence pieces and six 2 ps. Once they counted it up, which took several goes as they kept coming to different answers, they now had an additional £2.72. That meant they had £24 and 26 pence altogether. This was still nowhere near enough!

Pirate Terrance, aka Red Beard, had moved just a little bit further away from the others. He didn't need to search his pockets because he knew that in his secret pocket were two crisp new £20 notes. He tried to looked like he was doing nothing, but he was thinking. He was thinking about what he could do with his £40. He imagined getting the Gold Liner bus to Belfast. He pictured himself phoning some of his piratey friends, getting them to wire him a plane ticket. He imagined flying to Lanzarote and there joining a new pirate crew, a pirate crew with a ship. He could just slip away; slip away from the embarrassment; slip away from his old life; slip away to new adventures. But it wouldn't be good for the others, they'd be a man, £40, and a ship down, and all of this would be because of him!

His conscience pricked him. At first it was only a little tiny prick, so small it could be ignored. But it dug in a bit deeper, and eventually it couldn't be ignored. It reminded him, in a very annoying way that he was the one who hadn't tied the ship up properly; that he hadn't checked his knots; that he hadn't listened to Grey Beard when he had tried to teach him how to tie knots. In fact he had kept telling Grey Beard in a really cheeky voice, *"I know how to do that!"* when he had no idea at all. He remembered that he only ever practiced when Captain Timmy made him, and when he did, he did as little as possible!

Pirate Terrance, aka Red Beard made his decision. Quietly he slipped away from the other pirates. No one noticed him go. When a bit of a distance away and in mid slip, he shouted, *"I've found £40!"* The other pirates were just so relieved that they didn't ask where exactly he had found it, and instead cheered with joy. But Captain

Timmy and Grey Beard didn't cheer. While the other pirates thought this meant the boat was as good as rescued, Captain Timmy knew that it wasn't, and that this was only the start of all the hard work.

The Eighth Bit

Captain Timmy gave the secret signal for the pirates to gather. But none of them noticed the secret signal they're always meant to be looking for. He tried again, this time giving a discreet wave along with the secret signal. Again they didn't notice a thing! Next Captain Timmy accompanied the secret signal and discreet wave with a loud *"psssst"*. Yet again none of them noticed. In exasperation Captain Timmy roared at the top of his voice, *"Pirates, get over here now so I can tell you the secret plan!"* He shouted so loudly that people eating ice cream in their cars that were parked some distance away, stopped in mid lick to see who had shouted something or other about a secret plan!

Finally the pirates gathered around while the people in their cars returned to the licking of their ice cream. Captain Timmy now revealed his plan. The first part was obvious: they needed to get out of Portrush. Now that they had enough money, this part of the plan would be simple, though Captain Timmy had to keep warning them that danger loomed around every corner. They had damaged so many boats that everyone in Portrush, not just the irate boat owners were looking for them. Some people just wanted a selfie, famous or infamous was all the same to them, but still people were on the look-out for them.

At this point they were still okay for no one had seen them so couldn't describe them! But there was a real danger they'd been caught on CCTV, or video, or a camera phone. If such footage existed of them leaving the Bobbing Barrel, and if it appeared on social media, they would not be okay, in fact they'd be very un-okay!

Captain Timmy's plan involved getting the train to Coleraine. This wasn't so much genius on the part of the illustrious Captain. Instead this was their only option. After all, the little man with the meticulous moustache had told them that the police wouldn't be looking for them there, and it was his words that had planted the idea in Captain Timmy's mind!

The second part of the plan was the important part. They needed to get ahead of the Bobbing Barrel on land so they could see where it was at sea. From Coleraine the crew would split up and then head back to the coastline to try and catch a glimpse of the ship. If they did, they would then have to use all their piratey skills to recapture the vessel. This wouldn't be easy; actually it would be a very tricky, a nigh on impossible operation that was pretty much doomed to failure from the very start. But it was all they had so all they could do!

There was a third reason for going to Coleraine and not Portstewart, Castlerock, Ballycastle or

Ballintoy. This was a top secret reason. This was a reason that none of the pirates were told. There were stories, very vague and mysterious stories that in ancient times pirates had sailed up the Bann (by mistake) and settled in Coleraine (because their boat had got stuck trying to turn). Even pirates in the dim distant past did silly things just like pirates in the present day!

These ancient and mysterious stories recounted the establishment of a Moored Pirate cottage. You may well never have heard of a Moored Pirate Cottage as they're top secret, but Moored Pirate Cottages are very important places. Pirates meet in them and exchange code books, maps, or the names and locations of people who make piratey sort of things. Pirates are even duty bound to behave when inside one!

None of the pirates, or anyone else for that matter, knew if this cottage actually existed. But Coleraine was the sort of place a Moored Cottage would be located. Coleraine is a port. Yes that is correct. Coleraine is a port because it has a port.

So having a Moored Cottage in a port that no one thinks of as being a port is a great place to hide a Moored Cottage. Even one started by pirates who got their boat stuck!

As they set off for the train station, Captain Timmy tried to put out of his mind that he was really pinning all his hopes on two long shots. Their immediate challenge was simple though: get to the train station quickly. The train, or as some of them had started calling it, *'the escape vessel'* was leaving soon. They sprinted, then they jogged, then they briskly walked, the pace constantly slowing. Then, gasping for breath they sat down on someone's wall for a rest. With a further combination of sprinting, jogging, brisk walking but mostly slow walking, all of which was accompanied with lots of puffing and panting, they made it to the train station in the nick of time.

They rushed onto the train, but the guard threw them off for they hadn't got their tickets. They rushed to the ticket window. Here, Pirate Tattie banged into Pirate Terry, who banged into Pirate Terrance aka Red Beard, who banged into Grey Beard, who banged into Captain Timmy, who banged his head off the window, who was told off by the person selling the tickets to be more careful. Finally, the group ticket to Coleraine was purchased and they rushed onto the train. As they sank down into their seats, the doors closed and the train moved off. Mightily relieved, they watched through the train window as Portrush and all the chaos was smoothly left behind!

The Ninth Bit

The rhythmical movement of the train instantly
lulled the pirates to sleep. Like joyous children in
fancy dress they snoozed their way to Coleraine.
That is everyone except Grey Beard. It wasn't
that he was keeping watch. Rather his leisure
time in the Port had been sitting in a coffee shop
drinking coffee. Over the course of two hours
he'd drunk four flat whites (that's eight
espressos), and along with these he'd eaten four
huge tray bakes, and I do mean huge!

Looking out on the station as they approached
Coleraine, the pirates thought they had entered a
nightmare! Everywhere they looked, and I mean

everywhere they looked, there were hundreds and thousands of pirates lurking and lingering. There were big pirates and small pirates, tall pirates and short pirates, old pirates and young pirates, boy pirates and girl pirates, there was every style and size of pirate you could imagine, and they were absolutely everywhere! Captain Timmy and his crew decided that they were so badly outnumbered that they would stay on the train and come up with a plan. But the conductor was having none of it and turfed them off! His shift was nearly over and it had been a very long and hot day. He just wanted to get home, so this motley crew weren't going to keep him back.

Captain Timmy and Grey Beard who had been pirates forever (that is well over thirty years) didn't recognise a single one of them. In fact none of them even looked in the slightest bit similar to anyone they knew. After a good bit of gawking, Grey Beard spotted someone who looked a little bit like the Honourable Captain T Toms, that notorious English pirate.

The Honourable Captain T Toms, that notorious English pirate, and Grey Beard had had many run-ins over the years and were definitely not friends. They had fought about everything: from treasure to trifle. Once at a banquet in a rather fancy restaurant, they'd both wanted the last extra bowl of trifle, even though they'd had three already! They had started to debate about who should have it, but this quickly moved on to arguing, which was slightly embarrassing given the grandeur of their surroundings. Then they started to push, pull and shove each other. This jostling was not good at all. The battle was only averted when the hotel manager stepped in. He told them it was pitiable to fight over an extra pudding. Well, what he actually had said to them was that it was pitiable for them to fight over an extra pudding at their age and that they should both catch themselves on!

The manager of the fancy restaurant also warned them in no uncertain terms that if they didn't stop they'd both be thrown out. Thankfully in the end the only thing thrown out was the extra pudding!

But here on the streets of Coleraine, every step brought the pair closer and closer together. Grey Beard gritted his teeth. He prepared to apologise, to eat humble pie. He now wished he'd just given him the extra trifle. For now they needed help, even help from the likes of the Honourable Captain T Toms, that notorious English pirate. But when Grey Beard got near enough to see the whites of his eyes, it wasn't him, it was someone else, someone Grey Beard had never seen before.

Next it was Captain Timmy's turn to see someone he thought he knew: McNasty the Terrible, the infamous Welsh pirate. Yes, he was a Welsh pirate and not Scottish, although everyone thought he was. Once, long ago on a school trip to Scotland in P5, he started to call everything Mc this, Mc that, and Mc the other thing. Then miraculously within a few days he had acquired a Scottish accent that never went away!

Unlike Grey Beard and the Honourable Captain T Toms, that notorious English pirate, they got on well and had even helped each other out on a few occasions. But mores the pity, it wasn't him either!

Pirate Terrance, aka Red Beard was never shy and now determined he needed to know what was going on. As his curiosity reached bursting point, a lady stopped right beside him. Taking this as a sign, he grasped his golden opportunity. Pirate Terrance, aka Red Beard had noticed all the pirates, and he had noticed the woman who had stopped beside him, but he did miss a few rather important things. The woman was not alone. She had four children. There were three boys, all of whom were fighting with each other, and a baby girl who had just cried herself to sleep. All this while her husband was standing a short distance away, intently talking to a man he'd briefly worked with 15 years ago and not taking notice that the little boys were fighting, or that the little girl had been crying.

In his most posh accent, Pirate Terrance, aka Red Beard said, *"Excuse me madam"*. The lady stopped and the baby, though still sleeping, whimpered (never a good sign). He went on, *"Would you mind telling me what is going on today?"* With an incredulous look she replied, *"It's the pirate fancy dress competition. Did you not notice all the pirates?"* In this brief conversation, during which the baby woke up and started to cry quietly (the normal prelude to crying loudly) he also learned that the prizes were about to be given out in front of the town hall. Having told Captain Timmy, they moved along with the crowd to the prize giving.

Captain Timmy was unnerved. He'd never seen the like of it. His heart was thumping. Little beads of sweat formed on his brow, rolled down his face to his chin and then dripped onto the ground. All a bit gross really! For the pirates this was the most terrifying spectacle they had ever seen. Their past adventures would have stretched normal people to their limits. Yet this, a sea of fancy dress pirates was too much for them!

Within half a mile, in any direction you chose to look, were thousands of pirates!

Captain Timmy wanted to believe Pirate Terrance, aka Red Beard, but what if it wasn't true? What then? Thousands of pirates against a boatless band of brigands? No thank you, thought Captain Timmy! They had no option, they had to keep moving, to keep looking, to keep trying to be inconspicuous, which wasn't that hard, given that everyone was dressed up to look like a pirate!

Captain Timmy was valiantly trying to look calm and in total command. But his emotions were quivering. His heroic boldness was in short supply. So to help his thinking he kept repeating the mantra, "*These are not real pirates. These are not real pirates. These are not real pirates.*"

But as his mind drifted, it filled with thoughts of the surrounding lookalike pirates. Then, accidently his mantra changed, just a little, but now he was repeating, "*These are not real pirates.*

But they look like real pirates. These are not real pirates. But they look like real pirates."

Then, with another slip, he started to recite, "These look like real pirates so they might be real pirates. These look like real pirates so they might be real pirates." But thankfully, for him and the crew, before he started saying "These are real pirates" he managed to snap out of it!

The Tenth Bit

Captain Timmy, as captain, was meant to spot the dangers and the opportunities. But at this moment of time, and given his nervous tension caused by all the fancy dress pirates, he was doing neither! The pirates just followed the crowd all the way to the Town Hall. For once, they were happy and relieved, not standing out like a sore thumb!

As soon as they arrived in the square, something else caught their attention. All around its edge were pirate flags gently fluttering in the breeze. Upon closer inspection, they noticed that below each flag was a stall selling piratey type stuff!

With nosiness fully engaged they went to have a closer look. At first Captain Timmy was excited but this didn't last long for everything was made from plastic. He picked up a telescope that had no lenses and was made of plastic. He picked up a sword but it was also made of plastic, and was blunt! He saw a map, but it wasn't real. Everything was useless for real pirates. He was very disappointed! Grey Beard found a stall selling piratey type memorabilia, but it too was all fake! The other pirates found stalls that were selling very swanky pirate themed chocolates and sweeties. But with no money and no free samples, they had no idea if the real sweets tasted as good as they looked!

There was one stall that was selling something real and useful - the local newspaper! Local papers are great because they take interest in local news. But for the pirates that day it was a problem, the big local news story, the one that was written in big letters on a big poster read,

"Mysterious ship sinks four boats in Portrush Harbour."

Nervously the pirates gave the stall a wide berth, all except for Pirate Tattie who kept reading:

"Abandoned ship breaks lines and causes £1m+ of damage."

"Yacht owner calls those responsible 'dangerous idiots'."

"Police ask public to report anything strange or unusual to their answering machine."

"Mayor says: report vessel's location to coast guard so they can scuttle it."

Having quickly read, and then slowly re-read the headlines to let it all sink in, Pirate Tattie found the others and told them both the good and the bad news. The good news was that no one knew who had caused the damage, and the bad news was that everyone was being encouraged to look for them.

One by one the pirates sensed the same eerie feeling that they were being watched. Even Pirate Terrance, aka Red Beard, the one who normally noticed very little felt prickly!

Without delay Grey Beard started to scan the crowd. He was perhaps the greatest spotter pirate of his generation, though admittedly he had missed the untied knot - something that really annoyed him - something that he didn't mention just in case he inadvertently pointed out that he hadn't noticed!

His instincts were incredible. He noticed just about everything, and what he didn't notice he had the uncanny ability to sense. But over the years he'd also spent many hours training. Grey Beard saw what you ignored. He heeded what you paid no attention to. To him the seemingly unimportant was investigated and nothing was overlooked. Put simply, he saw the things that would save a pirate from danger.

He looked to the left, and then he looked to the right. His eyes danced over the faces of the men, the women and the children who thronged the square. He looked for something, for anything that was out of place, or even just a little bit odd, but there was nothing. Grey Beard wondered if he'd been wrong. Had his senses let him down? Was no one watching them? Had they just been overly anxious? Were their minds playing tricks on them?

Captain Timmy was first to notice him. He was a small well dressed man with a meticulous moustache who was standing between two stalls, staring straight at them. Grey Beard couldn't see the small well dressed man with the meticulous moustache because of where he had deliberately positioned himself. Then, with great purpose the small well dressed man with the meticulous

moustache stepped forward, just a little, just
enough to allow Grey Beard to catch a fleeting
glimpse of him, and then he was gone!

Captain Timmy, nervously whispered to Grey
Beard, *"Did you see him?"* *"Do you mean the little
chap who wasn't dressed like a pirate?"* Grey Beard
whispered back. *"Oh dear,"* Captain Timmy
sighed, *"So you saw him too!"* Then, even more
ominously, he went on, *"Did you see his badge?
The one of a little blue house."* On hearing this,
Grey Beard replied, *"Should we tell the others?"*
The little blue house was a very secret pirate sign,
one which might have to do with a Moored
Cottage, but nobody knew for sure if that's what
it actually meant!

The Eleventh Bit

Captain Timmy gave the order to slip away. The order took a good while to make its way down the line, and needed to be repeated several times. But once they'd started the slipping away bit, their slipping away was very good. Their next problem was waiting for them when they arrived at the place they'd slipped off to. There he was, leaning against a lamp post and looking straight at them again - the small well dressed man with the meticulous moustache. So without a chance to regroup, and with no other option, they had to slip off again.

However, they soon discovered that they were trying to out slip someone who was far more slippery than them. Someone who possessed far greater piratey skills than they did! Someone who wasn't going to be easily slipped away from, if at all. No matter which direction they tried to slip off in, and believe me they tried to slip away in every imaginable direction, he was always ahead of them, gazing straight at them, notebook in hand! Then, as they were looking at him, he seemed to vanish! They all heaved a great sigh of relief.

When they were sure that he was really gone, they felt much less threatened and their nosiness returned remarkably quickly. This part of the pirate festival concluded with the prize giving and they wanted to see who had won what, and if they deserved their reward or not! They also had a bit of time to kill before splitting up and going off in search of their ship, for once the trophies had been handed out, most of the people would start heading home. This would mean that there would be look-a-like pirates heading in every direction. It would be much easier to blend in if they just waited a wee while!

But when they got to the prize giving, there he was, on the stage, looking straight at them yet again - the small well dressed man with the meticulous moustache! He was the only person in the entire crowd who didn't look like a pirate. As he was also the only person in the entire crowd with the proficiency and expertise of a pirate, which gave them the distinct impression that he could be one! A pirate who was keeping a very close eye on them.

The microphone started making loud squealing noises for the volume was too high. A disinterested trainee sound engineer ambled over and turned it down, whereupon the strange noises stopped. Next, a rather official looking woman who was wearing a big gold chain around her neck, stepped forward to the microphone.

The mayor, because that's who the lady was, gave all the normal welcomes. Then she went on, *"This year we have a new prize. One that was only thought of this morning. In fact it was only thought of as news of those awful events in Portrush harbour were starting to come through."* She stooped and sighed deeply. Then with composure recaptured she continued, *"We have a new category, 'mystery pirate fancy dress for adults'. As you know, all the other categories must be entered, but not this one. Instead Mr Humphreys has been our top-secret judge."* As she said this she looked straight at the small well dressed man with the meticulous moustache, who we should note had not taken his eyes off Captain Timmy! *"He was the one who came up with the idea for this new category. So, without further ado the inaugural winners are…"* Then, having given an appropriately long pause for theatrical affect, she pointed straight at Captain Timmy!

Once the polite applause, which didn't last very long, had died down she continued, *"Congratulations! I must say you're the most realistic looking pirates I've ever seen! Thank you for trying so hard!"* Then, as they hadn't moved, she waved for Captain Timmy to come to the stage and said, *"Please come up and get your prize."*

Captain Timmy was shocked. But he was also beaming from ear to ear with a huge smile, as though they'd meant to win the prize - a prize they knew nothing about! On the stage, having shaken hands and received another *'well done,'* the mayor pinned the first place rosette on Captain Timmy's lapel. Next she handed Mr Humphries an envelope that he presented to Captain Timmy without a smile or a well done. However, unnoticed by absolutely everyone, the envelope that the mayor had given him had been slipped into his pocket, and a different envelope that looked exactly the same replaced it! Mr Humphries, still unsmiling, shook hands with Captain Timmy, who froze as he whispered to him, *"You won't lose this, or let it drift away, will you?"*

Once the official photographs had been taken, they went round the back of the stage and opened the envelope.

First was a book token for £10, for a local bookshop none of them had ever heard of. Even when they checked on the World Wide Web it wasn't mentioned. Stranger still, the bookshop was only open on Tuesday mornings between 11 am and 12 noon and the book token was only valid for one week!

Second was a travel pass for the 'Triangle' - that's Coleraine, where they were; Portrush, where they had lost their boat; and Portstewart which was up the coast from Portrush.

Third was an, eat all you can voucher for a fancy ice cream shop in Portstewart, and it was only valid for today.

Fourthly was a microlight flight for two people, leaving Portstewart Strand in exactly one hour.

Written beside it in very neat hand writing were the words, *"Don't miss the flight or else!"*

The Twelfth Bit

Finally things seemed to be looking up. But the pirates needed to get to Portstewart, and quickly. So they headed straight to the bus station. Grey Beard, the potency of the four flat whites now wearing off, was feeling tired and groggy. It was in this diminished state that he nearly made a calamitous mistake. The Portrush Town Service and the Portstewart Express buses were parked beside each other. Grey Beard didn't read the signs properly so he directed the crew onto the wrong bus! Once on board they sat down. The bus was warm, the seats soft, and a sense of safety swept over the pirates. One by one they started to fall asleep. They thought they were heading for Portstewart and free ice cream, and they were happy. Very happy. Very, very happy. Far too happy!

Then something very annoying happened. Two older men got on the bus and sat right in front of Captain Timmy and Grey Beard. They'd come over to Coleraine from Mosside to see the festivities. They started talking, talking very loudly. Captain Timmy and Grey Beard could hear every word spoken. It wasn't so much that they were eavesdropping, it was just that they couldn't ignore them! But what they were talking about suddenly became important when they mentioned the incident at Portrush harbour. Captain Timmy and Grey Beard stopped trying to ignore and started listening intently. They covered all the normal things: *"a runaway boat"*; *"an incompetent captain"*; *"it wasn't tied up properly you know"*; *"they still haven't been caught"*; *"we still don't know who did it"* and so on. Their interest started waning. That is, until the men mentioned a crane toppling into the harbour as it tried to lift a boat out. Thankfully the driver hadn't been injured! Then came the important part. They talked about having to get off the bus at the railway station, and that it would be a *"brave dander doon tha toon til hae a wee duke, befaire ait's ail red up."* It took a wee while for them to comprehend what they were hearing, but when the penny dropped they realised they were on the wrong bus!

Quickly - that is as quickly as they could wake up all the pirates and get them to change buses - they changed buses. The instant they got onto the Portstewart Express, it swept out of the bus station, five minutes late. None of them noticed, but the driver was a small well dressed man with a meticulous moustache who had his hat pulled right down over his face! In no time at all Captain Timmy and Grey Beard were on Portstewart Strand. The bus (this had never happened before, nor since) drove right down onto the Strand and they got off! Then it took the rest of the pirates straught to the door of the swanky ice cream parlour. No one noticed, but they hadn't asked to be left off there.

On the Strand the waves were crashing, the sun was shining and the microlights were waiting. The two pirates listened to the safety briefing, a safety briefing they had to receive several times as Captain Timmy kept asking questions about crashing, and what to do if you crashed, and if the pilots had ever crashed before, and he kept telling them that he would not like to crash.

Eventually they put on their flight suits and helmets. Having been shown to their seats, they were strapped in. Before leaving, the pilot explained that the flight would follow the coastline and that it would last as long as it needed to. She also told them that if they spotted anything really important they were to tell her and she would land. Though absolutely terrified, Captain Timmy couldn't help thinking this was the perfect way to search for their ship. So simultaneously he was petrified and excited.

The pilot, noticing Captain Timmy's continuing fear, the gritted teeth and grimaced face, shouted over the roar of the engine, *"You're as safe as houses!"* Giving the harness one last tug, she said, *"You're going to love this Captain. I'll make it the experience of a lifetime!"* Then she took her seat and strapped on her own harness.

Likewise, Captain Timmy thought this would be the experience of a lifetime. That is he thought it would be an extremely bad experience! At sea Captain Timmy was fearless. He would merrily face any enemy, storm, or danger. He would face down a dozen fierce pirate ships. He would happily lead the Royal Navy on a merry dance. However, this going up into the sky carry on, it seemed to him and his sea legs like utter madness. But worse still, it seemed to him to be dangerous! Floating and flying were just not the same thing.

Captain Timmy was the captain, and being the captain meant responsibility: responsibility for the ship, for its crew, even for the one who hadn't tied it up properly. So whether he liked it or not it was his duty to fly! He clenched his fists. He gritted his teeth even harder. He told himself everything would be okay, even though he didn't believe a word of it. Captain Timmy knew the pilot had never crashed. He knew this because he'd asked her a dozen times. On each occasion the answer was always '*no*'! It started as a simple no, but in the end it had become pretty emphatic. The last time Captain Timmy asked (which was over the radio, so he couldn't see the smile) she answered, "*No I've never crashed, but I suppose there's a first time for everything!*" Captain Timmy didn't reply as he was too scared to say another word! But it was all he could think about!

The Thirteenth Bit

The engine now produced a powerful revving sound. Then it fell back just a little, then revved even further, then fell back again. Over and over it repeated this until finally they shot down the beach and up into the sky. Unlike Captain Timmy, Grey Beard loved the idea of flying! He couldn't wait to get up into the sky to look down on the world below. On the Bobbing Barrel, Grey Beard loved to climb the foremast, or the mizzenmast, or best of all up into the crow's nest. He was always mesmerized by the view. Now all he could think, as they fired down the beach, was how much better the view would be from the sky! But he also trusted the skill and experience of the skipper, whether it was a ship on the high sea or an aircraft high in the sky.

When the bouncing stopped, Captain Timmy knew they were in the sky. That was the only reason he knew as his eyes were tightly shut and he could see nothing. In fact he'd seen nothing since the quip about, *"...a first time for everything!"*

Quickly they cleared the mouth of the River Bann, and then Castlerock came and went. Next the ruins of Downhill appeared ahead of them. The pilot, talking over the crackly radio asked, *"We can take a better look at Mussenden Temple if you want?"* Grey Beard, getting into the spirit of the flight replied, *"Roger that Captain!"* Captain Timmy said nothing, but in a few minutes, he wished he had said something! Something like, *'No thank you'*, or *'Please don't do that!'*

Since the mouth of the Bann, the microlights had flown over the edge of the land. To the left (the port side) while the water was to the right (the starboard side). Without changing course, they flew past Mussenden Temple. Captain Timmy, who had momentarily opened his eyes, was mightily relieved. He thought they'd changed their minds and flown on. Then suddenly, and without any warning, the aircraft banked hard to the left. They were now flying at a 45° angle (that's halfway between lying down and standing up). If a ship slanted that much it would sink, and this was all Captain Timmy could think! But Grey Beard thought it was the most amazing thing he had seen in his entire life! Captain Timmy thought it was unspeakably horrific. The pilots didn't think about it at all. It was just the kind of thing they did for excited tourists (like Grey Beard), or to give nervous fliers (like Captain Timmy) a little bit of a scare!

They flew around Mussenden Temple in a great big loop, all the way banking hard at 45°! This gave a spectacular view of the scenery below though Captain Timmy didn't see much as his eyes were tightly shut again. Once the loop was finished and balance restored, they went back to flying over the edge of the land. Soon they flew over the long and sandy beach at Downhill. Then they flew over Benone. Some children waved up from the camping site below. Captain Timmy, whose eyes were actually open now, saw the children waving. He didn't wave back for he couldn't bring himself to let go of the handrail he was tightly gripping. Next they flew over Magilligan Point. Below were some strange looking buildings with lots of fences, walls and lights.

Clearing the headland they banked left. To keep up with nautical terminology, that is they banked hard to port side. They now headed down Lough Foyle flying high above it. Below them a small car ferry was making its way from one side to the other. The tide was out, revealing the mud banks along the shore. To their left was farm land with great big hills behind it - Binevenagh. Captain Timmy was still not happy but he had managed to keep his eyes open. Even he had to admit there was an amazing view from up here though he still found the whole experience totally terrifying.

He later described flying as being like walking into a cave and accidentally finding a sleeping dragon, something amazing but something you'd be better not doing!

They flew across the water to Greencastle, and from here they headed down Lough Foyle along the Donegal shore. Then Grey Beard saw it in the distance - their ship - somehow or other washed up on a little beach just above Moville towards Greencastle!

The Fourteenth Bit

The microlights they were travelling in had been specially adapted to land on water. Along with wheels they had great big long floats! Being able to land on the ground or on the sea would be very helpful if you had a lost ship to rescue. Grey Beard didn't want to say too much. He didn't want to give the game away. By blurting out, *"That's our ship down there! The one we lost!"* But he needed to say something, so speaking over the radio, Grey Beard nervously said, *"Hmmmmm. Do you see the ship on the beach?"* Calmly the pilot replied, *"Yes I see the pirate ship that is washed up on the beach down there. The one that drifted here from Portrush. It's pretty hard to miss!"* Captain

Timmy, speaking for the first time since becoming airborne asked, *"Could we. . .well. . .eh you know. . .land beside it?"* Instantly the pilot replied, *"Roger that."*

This shocked Captain Timmy. Not in his wildest dreams had he thought she'd say yes! It just goes to show you that it's always worth asking, for the worst that can be said is 'no'! The pilots, having relayed instructions to one another, changed course and flew out over the water. They then turned around, aimed inland and slowed the speed of the engines. The aircraft started to lower in the sky but something strange happened as they slowed down. As they got closer to the water it seemed as though they were speeding up. Down and down they went, closer and closer to the water they got, but quicker and quicker they seemed to go!

This was scary for the pirates. Even Grey Beard didn't like it! Ten feet above the water, six feet, two feet, a few inches, and then they bounce, bounce, bounced along the lough! They kept moving until they were on the beach. The microlights, were turned around, aimed out to the lough and made ready for takeoff before they came to a halt. The engines were then switched off and their seat belts released!

Now taking a huge risk, Grey Beard said, *"This is our ship and we need to get it afloat."* *"Okay,"* the pilot replied, *"We've done this kind of thing before. Though it was normally caused by storms not an untied rope!"* Grey Beard was very surprised but again said nothing. The pilot walked around the Bobbing Barrel and then came back to them. *"The tide's coming in pretty quickly, so if we make the boat a bit lighter, and then raise the sails at the right time, I think we should get it free on our own, without commandeering the tug boat from Greencastle."*

Captain Timmy and Grey Beard rushed up the ladder and started to throw things over the edge. But the Pilot rather crossly shouted at them to stop. She climbed up into the ship while the other pilot stayed with the aircraft (they were no fools, they weren't going to lose a microlight)!

Once on board she told them to put the heaviest things into cargo nets, and then drop them onto the sand at the seaward side of the Bobbing Barrel. She had to remind them that they actually needed the things they were throwing overboard, something that had completely gone out of Captain Timmy and Grey Beard's minds! If they used the cargo nets, once they were afloat they could winch them back onboard. Also they wouldn't pollute the Foyle with all their junk!

The tide was now racing in extremely quickly, so they worked hard, harder than they had worked in a very long time! Everything that needed to go overboard was heavy and clumsy! Finally, the last cargo net was thrown overboard and splashed into the lough. Captain Timmy and Grey Beard flopped onto the deck, totally exhausted. But the pilot shouted at them, *"Get up lazy bones, you have to raise the sails!"* Captain Timmy was about to give the order, *"Raise the main sail!"* but then he remembered he and Grey Beard needed to do it themselves! Furiously they started to hoist the sails. No sooner were they up

than the wind caught them and they were free!
Once again Captain Timmy was the captain of
the Bobbing Barrel. . .that was at last bobbing
again!

The pilot said, as she climbed down the ladder,
*"Pirates, you should be okay on your own. Go and
collect your crew then come back and hoist up the
cargo nets. If you're quick you should be back in time
for the high tide."* The microlights engines revved,
they shot across the water and then into the sky,
down the lough, and disappeared out of sight.

The Bobbing Barrel was creaking and groaning,
just like Captain Timmy and Grey Beard. But it
also was moving freely, unlike Captain Timmy
and Grey Beard. They quickly, well as quickly as
they could, sailed to Portstewart.

Captain Timmy and Grey Beard did a remarkable
job sailing the Bobbing Barrel back to
Portstewart. Never once was an order shouted, a
chastisement given, a command explained. They
knew exactly what they needed to do, and they
just did it, the way they'd been taught. They had

to work very hard as there were only two of them, and they were getting really tired as it had been a long day. But they managed the short distance without further incident! Once they got to Portstewart and the Bobbing Barrel was just outside the harbour, they dropped the anchor and **tied** the lines. Captain Timmy tied the knots and Grey Beard checked them - that was how it was meant to be done - the way they didn't do in Portrush! Once they were absolutely sure the ship was tied, a little rowing boat was dropped into the water. Then Grey Beard, having unsteadily climbed down the rope ladder, rowed to the harbour...while Captain Timmy stayed with the ship...just in case!

The ice cream shop was on the Main Street so had a great view out to sea, but none of the crew had noticed the Bobbing Barrel sailing past! The very second Grey Beard walked into the ice cream shop, totally unsure how he would get the crew out, a small well dressed man with a meticulous moustache, and a baseball cap pulled down over his face, (someone who had seen the Bobbing Barrel sail by,) appeared behind the counter. He picked up a microphone, and announced over the speakers in a very authoritative tone, that the shop was now shut, and that everyone must leave straight away, and anyone who had won an eat-all-you-can token could take their ice cream, their bowls, spoons, drinks and whatever else with them – which of course they did!

Once the crew were back on the Bobbing Barrel and the cargo nets retrieved (which took a while, as they had eaten so much ice cream), they sailed off to the high seas. Once the north coast was out of sight, Captain Timmy brought the book token out of his pocket and looked at it. He said to Grey Beard, *"I think we're going to have to go back on Tuesday and use this..."*

The End
Or is it?

Printed in Great Britain
by Amazon